Short Stories and Poetry by a South African

Written by

Sevani Singaram

Verity Publishers
Pretoria

Short Stories
and Poetry
by a
South African

Published in the Republic of South Africa

Short Stories and Poetry by a South African

This edition is published in paperback
©2022
in the Republic of South Africa
Copyright ©2022
Verity Publishers
Pretoria 0001
www.veritypublishers.co.za

ISBN 978-1-990985-28-7

Cover Design by Melvyn Naidoo

Table of Contents
❧

PART ONE (Poetry)

PART TWO (SHORT STORIES)

1
DURBAN IS HOME
☙❧

𝑀y ancestors came to Durban from India in 1860
They travelled on the Truro by sea.
Hundreds of years later, I was born in Durban,
a city that is scenic, vibrant and 'oh so urban.'
As a teenager, my favourite hangout was The Workshop or
the Wheel,
where I would often enjoy a bunny chow, which made a
delicious meal.
I pursued tertiary studies at the Durban University of
Technology.
It was there that I studied radiography.
After graduating I was employed at King Edward Hospital,
a large public medical facility.
Presently, I work at a private clinic, which is not too far from
the city.

Durban is my home and where my heart will always be.
From the calming ocean to bustling Blue Lagoon, it is where
I am most free.
From the Moses Mabhida Stadium to Mitchell Park,
From Suncoast Casino to the Umgeni River Bird Park.
There's something for everyone to enjoy, in the light or dark.

A culinary adventure awaits all those in Durban.
You can tantalise your taste buds with Cornish curry, fried mealies or puttu and curry,
and if you are lucky, deep fried sardines will satisfy any rumbling tummy.
I am proudly South African and even prouder to call Durban my home.

2
COVID-19
ॐ

The world is practicing social distancing, to stop the spread
of COVID-19
Economies are collapsing and people are dying,
All while millions of people are starving
Health workers are on the frontline, working tirelessly to
save lives
They are putting patients first in so many instances,
If it weren't for them, there would be many more fatalities
Scientists are working on a cure or vaccine, as infected
people are forced to go into quarantine
But as the virus threatens livelihoods, nations are uniting for
a common goal
Aid is being sent to needy countries, and for now, most
countries show no hostility
The earth is healing since there is less pollution
It took a virus to temporarily sort out the pollution situation
We don't know if life will ever return to normal, perhaps we
need to embrace a new normal,
But one thing is for certain, we now have a newfound
appreciation for our lives in general.

3
BORN TO LEAD
∾

At just fifteen years, Letti is pregnant.
The scorn and outrage from family and friends is imminent.
The father of the child refuses to accept responsibility,
and thinks of Letti and her unborn child as a liability.
But despite this, Letti is determined to finish her schooling,
because she wants a better life for herself and her kin.
Letti delivers the baby on a raging stormy night.
The raging storm gives the baby a fright.
It's a gorgeous girl, and Letti wants to give her the world.
Letti's mother reluctantly watches the baby while Letti
studies.
She shouts out to Letti "Will you please hurry ?"
Two years later, Letti completes matric.
She feels as though she has scored a hat trick.
With no money to go to university,
Letti starts waitressing to support herself and her baby.
The hours are long and gruesome.
Letti must deal with a male manager who is sometimes
intrusive.
He touches her neck and shoulders inappropriately.
Letti feels she can't voice her concerns because she needs the
money.

She enrols at a local college to study teaching through
correspondence,
And dreams of a world of abundance when she gains her
independence.

In a suburb not too far from Letti, lives Rekha and her
family.
An outsider would claim Rekha has the best life,
but few know how hard she has to strive.
Others envy Rekha because she is a lady of leisure,
but what Rekha endures, does not give her pleasure.
Behind closed doors Rekha's husband beats her.
He is an alcoholic and does not know how to treat her.
Rekha thinks this is the norm,
Her family chooses to ignore that she is forlorn.
While her children are at school Reka wishes she hadn't been
a fool.
She left school for her husband who promised her the world,
yet today she feels like his maid, without even a pearl.
The lipstick on his clothes are signs that he is having an
affair,
but when she questions him, he just beats her.
With no job or formal skill, Rekha is financially dependent
on this man.
Oh! how she wishes she was courageous and braver, just to
take a stand.
An advertisement in a newspaper catches her eye;
There is a receptionist vacancy, she wants to apply.

The interviewers commend Rekha's interest and enthusiasm to learn.

They decide to give her a chance.

Now, for the better, her life would change.

In another province, Doctor Renata Nel prides herself on saving lives;

Yet, many criticize her because she is not yet a wife.

She has been told that a lady should strive for marriage.

So, when she called off her engagement, it was met with outrage.

They didn't know that her ex-fiancée was like a parasite.

He would take her money and then vanish out of sight.

Renata wanted a better life partner;

But she was ridiculed for wanting better.

She was told that the older you get, you ought to settle for any man;

But for her 'settling' was never the plan.

Her friend's most famous line was, "What if you never get to experience motherhood?"

Renata quickly responded, "I just want to be happy. Is that understood?"

Renata was resilient, but sometimes the negative comments made her feel down;

She wouldn't want to leave her home and would watch television in her gown.

As a doctor, she knew the importance of looking after her mental health,

So she booked an appointment with a clinical psychologist,

recommended by a friend who was a psychiatrist.
The clinical psychologist enabled her to live her best life,
and that's just the gist.

Women, the world over, should be kind to one other;
for most of our needs and dreams are so similar.
We all yearn to be loved by our life partners, husbands or
boyfriends,
And we hope that their love for us never ends.
But, sometimes, life takes us on a different bend.
We hope to have the perfect children;
Some even treat their kids like a prized possession.
We fail to realise that it is impossible to have this type of
perfection.
We may look down on women who put their careers first or
strive for a better job in their company;
yet fail to realise that these women are making a significant
contribution to our economy.
Let's not judge women who don't have children;
You don't know her reasons and don't presume that she is
barren.
Don't ask a woman why she is not married;
This is a question laden with cynicism and sarcasm
Sometimes, it is meant to belittle unmarried women.

History reminds us that when women work together
something great is achieved;
Come on women, lets strengthen this belief.
After all, we were born to lead!

4

CLOUD NINE

On cloud nine is a perfect place to be
In fact, you will never want to leave
Once the euphoria hits you,
You're stuck to the cloud like glue
But! Beware
Once you come crashing down
It is inevitable that you will be forlorn
The highs and lows of life;
Can make it easier or harder to strive
For some cloud nine may seem out of reach
And they make resort to drugs
To stick to the cloud like a leech
For once you're on cloud nine
Everything is mighty fine
You will wish that time could stand still
Even if you have to take a pill
For on cloud nine is a perfect place to be.

5
QUARANTINE
∝⧵

The world has come to a halt,
Coronavirus is the cause.
I'm alone with my thoughts in quarantine,
and wonder if this is how God meant it to be.
For while the world pauses, mother nature is healing,
and there is a newfound appreciation for human interaction.
I will emerge out of quarantine a better person,
for I have pondered on life's lessons.

6
A POEM FOR MY MOTHER

𝔄 mother has many roles,
Teacher, chef, and nurse are just a few of the roles I'm told.
I am grateful for all that Mum has done for me,
She is the shining star in our family tree.
Friends may come and go,
But Mum is the truest friend I know.
I'm convinced Mum has a super power,
Because sometimes she can even make Dad cower.
When Mum gets old, I must remember to be patient with her,
For if it wasn't for her, I wouldn't be here.
I sympathise with those who have lost their mothers,
They are missing out on a love like no other.
My Mum will always have a special place in my heart,
For she was there for me from the start.

7

SUNDAY

Sunday is my favourite day of the week
It is often the only day on which I am not bleak
I begin my day with an uplifting church service
And later on, I shop for my favourite things
But most of all, I love spending time with loved ones
Hugs, kisses and tasty meals are just what I want
It is for these reasons that I await Sunday all week long
And even if there is a Sunday on which I don't have much planned
I use the day to rest after six days of working hard.

8

3 AM

It's 3am and I'm wide wake
I'm supposed to be sleeping
But my mind won't take a break
I wish I could fall into a deep sleep
But my racing thoughts won't let me
I cannot hear any voices emanating from outside
And there is also silence in my abode
So then, why can't I fall asleep?
In my mind, I may have to count sheep
For in a few hours, my day will begin
And I can't be lethargic, because I have much to accomplish.

9
AFRICAN INDIAN
ॐ

I am a proud African Indian
I relate to Eastern and African nations
My forefathers arrived in South Africa in 1860
Because they wanted to carve a better life for their family
Many Indians in South Africa fought against apartheid
Some were killed, others were imprisoned,
Because they wanted injustices to end.

As I reflect on the last twenty-seven years of democracy
I realise that Indians have also contributed to the economy
They have started businesses, built schools and even opened
eateries
Indian cuisine is popular among many in Mzansi
A dish that is commonly enjoyed by all is rice and curry
And how can I forget the mouth-watering mutton bunny?
It's been known to fill many tummies.

South Africa is a resilient country
We have overcome many adversities
We are the epitome of a rainbow nation
And although we have much to learn and achieve
We should for a moment, rejoice in victory

I embrace both my African and Indian heritages
I have much to be proud of, don't you think?

10
ALONE

I'm alone but I'm not lonely
I'm comfortable not having company
When I'm left alone with my thoughts,
My mind is clearer and I am not distraught
I cherish meaningful conversations with like-minded people
But I tend to repel the complainers and those who are fickle
I do not rely on others to make me happy
Perhaps they might feel it is a huge responsibility
I am alone but I am not lonely.

11

NOSTALGIA

Once in a while, my mind transports me back in time
I think of what was seen, heard, tasted and felt
And I sometimes wish that I could relive that moment
I also wish that bad memories could be permanently erased
Removed! Gone! Forever deleted!
But we wouldn't appreciate the good times, if we didn't
endure bad times
Good times bring us happiness and bad times teach us
valuable lessons
So savour every moment, and let's not lament.

PART TWO
(SHORT STORIES)

12

PARALLEL LIVES
⚶

*L*esedi awakes from a bad dream. Perspiration drips from her face and she looks perturbed. With half opened eyes, she switches on the light. The light seems to ease her anxiety, like it did when she had nightmares as a child, and she sits on the edge of her king-size bed, contemplating life. She glances at her alarm. It's 4:15am. Two hours before she usually wakes up. She does not want to go back to bed. Bad dreams emotionally overwhelm her whenever there is a stressor. On this occasion, the stressor was her impending final law examination. Although her family was financially stable, and she could always depend on them for support, she did not want to disappoint her parents who had invested a large sum of money in her education.

Lesedi was the second child of Mr and Mrs Biyela, who were entrepreneurs. They ran a successful bakery, Biyela's Delights, in a busy commercial area. They were busiest in the mornings and at lunch time, when blue collar and white collar workers would come to buy coffee, Chelsea buns, snowballs and toasted sandwiches. When the workers asked them to add freshly made pies, burgers and hot dogs to the menu, Mrs Biyela did not refuse. Biyela's Delights employed seven females (four bakers, two cleaners and one cashier) and the Biyela's felt proud to contribute towards female empowerment.

Mr Biyela's father earned a living working as a principal and upon his death, Mr Biyela, an only son, inherited a fortune, much to the dismay of his sisters. The Biyela's palatial four-bedroom home in the affluent suburb of Umhlanga Rocks overlooked the Indian ocean. It was furnished with designer furniture collected from their travels locally and internationally. They were financially set for life, or so Lesedi thought.

Lesedi's older sister, affectionately known as Minnie, is a doctor in rural KwaZulu-Natal and is devoted to saving lives while improving access to healthcare for those from impoverished backgrounds. Minnie is the 'blue-eyed girl' of the family. She excelled in academics and sports, and passed her MBChB degree cum laude. When the smart and breathtakingly handsome, Dr. Moses Shabalala, a newly graduated neurosurgeon, asked Minnie to be his girlfriend, that was the cherry on top for her parents. Minnie and Moses were regarded as a power couple in their social circle.

Lesedi eyes the pile of books on her study table, but soon realises that trying to cram studying at the last minute, would be purposeless. It would overload her brain. She reluctantly gets out of bed and heads to her en-suite where she kept the anti-anxiety medication that her doctor prescribed a couple of days ago. Luckily for Lesedi, she does not have to share a bathroom with the rest of her family. Her parents were overprotective and overbearing, so she did not want to discuss her mental health problems with them.

Lesedi's well-respected doctor had warned her not to take the medication on an empty stomach, but Lesedi needs a quick remedy. There is also a slight tremor in her hands and she is weak at the knees. Her wooden bathroom cabinet houses her toiletries and a variety of hair care products, but there was still enough space at the back of the cabinet to hide the white bottle of Xanax. She swiftly takes one Xanax capsule with a sip of water and closes the cabinet door. The mirror mounted on the front of the cabinet reflects a grim Lesedi. Her eyes are puffy and her visible clavicles highlights her weight loss. Her once pearly white teeth are stained yellow due to her smoking. She started smoking in her first year of university to fit in with the in-crowd and has found it exceedingly difficult to kick the habit. Lesedi heads back to bed and when she awakes, it is 7am. One hour before her examination is due to commence. Although her parents gifted her with a red sports car on her birthday, she realises that even if she drives like a notorious speedster from a Fast and Furious movie, she would still be late!

Naledi's day begins at 4am. She lives in a modest two-bedroom home in a semi-rural town with her octogenarian grandmother and twin sisters who recently celebrated their eighth birthday. There is a list of chores that she needs to complete before heading off to university – making breakfast, sweeping, mopping and getting the twins ready for school. Luckily she is exempt from taking the twins to school because it is nearby and her neighbour performs this task as a favour to her. Her parents were killed in a taxi accident when the twins were three years old, rendering Naledi a pseudo adult.

Her grade eleven teacher, Mrs. Ntolo, recognised her intellectual gift and encouraged her to apply for a bursary. When Naledi was informed that she was a recipient of the bursary, she had insomnia for days because she was overcome with excitement. She would be the first person in her family to attend university which was a feat in itself.

Now, four years later, she is about to take her final law examination. It had been an exigent four years, but

Naledi's resilience and faith in God saw her through. Naledi's grandmother, affectionately called, Gogo, supported her grandchildren by using her meagre pension supplemented by baking for neighbours, family and friends. Gogo's vetkoek and mealie-bread were the talk of the neighbourhood. Everybody wanted to know what was Gogo's secret to making mouth-watering vetkoek and mealie-bread. Gogo was adamant that the secret was just love.

Naledi's immediate neighbours, the Celes, moved to Johannesburg when Mr. Cele was offered a higher paying job, and they still visited Gogo when they were in the neighbourhood. They even buy Gogo's delicacies to enjoy as *padkos*. By 6am, Naledi is at the taxi rank. She is exhausted from staying up late to study and waking up early to tend to the house and her siblings. She falls asleep at her window seat. Naledi is woken by the gentle nudge of a stocky old lady.

"Wake up dear. We are approaching your stop." Naledi thanks her and glances at her wristwatch. It is 7am. One hour before her examination. She prefers to be early, rather than late for any examination.

Naledi says a silent prayer before she opens her examination question sheet. Her prayer time is interrupted by shuffling at the entrance of the exam hall. She opens her eyes to find a panic stricken Lesedi looking for something in her brown Louis Vuitton bag. Although they attended the same lectures, they were not friends because once Lesedi made a joke about Naledi's worn out bag and shoes. Naledi fought back tears as she walked away from the group of girls who belonged to a higher social class just because they were wealthier than her.

"Hurt people hurt people. She obviously has a problem if she judges people based on what they wear," said Gogo when Naledi relayed the incident while shedding tears on her beloved grandmother's shoulders.

Gogo always knew how to put things into perspective for clarity. Naledi thought that sometimes, wisdom really does come with age.

When Lesedi can't find what she is looking for in her bag, she mumbles something to herself, stomps her feet and leaves the venue. She returns a few minutes later, looking more composed and with her stationery case in hand. Mrs Smith, the moderator, directs her to her seat. Lesedi opens the examination question sheet and closes it after taking a quick glance. She closes her eyes and takes a few deep breaths. The anti-anxiety medication that she took a few hours earlier is not working. She wishes she could leave the venue, but she does not want to disappoint her parents.

It is 6pm when Naledi arrives home. The taxi broke down and it took ages before another one arrived. The rush hour traffic did not help her plight. Naledi is fatigued, but she helps Gogo to prepare dinner by chopping the vegetables for stew. Meat was costly and was only cooked on a Sunday or when visitors arrived. Thereafter, she helps the twins with their homework. There is no time to ponder her last exam. There was also no time to meet friends or to have a social life like many of her peers. The twins and Gogo needed her help.

Lesedi arrives home just after 6pm. She headed to the Gateway Mall after the exam to de-stress. A shopping spree always made her feel better. This shopping trip, in particular, costed her R5,500. She treated herself to a Guess bag and heels from Aldo shoes. While traipsing through the mall, she bumped into Tina who was once her bestie. Shortly after high school, Tina unexpectedly fell pregnant and then had endless responsibilities. The most popular high school duo then lost contact with each other. Tina looked much older than twenty-four years and Lesedi would have not recognised her if Tina did not approach her with a greeting and hug. Lesedi was not aloof towards Tina. After all, they did not have a fall out, but just drifted apart because they were at different phases in their lives.

"It's good to see you," said Tina as she gave Lesedi a warm hug.

"Likewise. How are you and your little girl?" Lesedi asked, as she reciprocated the hug.

"I'm great thanks, and as for the little girl... She is now six years old," Tina laughed. "She is spending quality time with her dad, so I thought it would be ideal for me to do the weekly shopping." Lesedi eyed the Pick 'n Pay packets in Tina's trolley.

"If you are free now, let's catch up over coffee," said Lesedi.

Tina obliged and the two reminisced over their teenage years that now seemed like eons ago. They laughed about their follies in school and how they would prank their classmates. Weekends were spent at each other's homes, where they would try different hairstyles and makeup trends inspired by Cosmopolitan and Glamour magazines.

Once, Lesedi caused Tina to suffer a momentary chilli burn when she applied honey and chillies onto her face. Tina remembered that incident vividly. After two cups of coffee each and a slice of Bar-One and carrot cake, they decided to head home. The two exchanged cellphone numbers and promised to meet every few months.

As Lesedi past the famous Sue's Sensational Delights, a popular eatery, the aroma of their signature mutton stew wafted through the air. Lesedi couldn't resist and decided to get a takeaway. When she arrived home, her parents were gone out to dinner with friends, so Lesedi ate the mutton stew in the comfort of her room. If her parents were home, they would insist that they ate dinner together. They cherished family time.

It was three weeks until the release of the final examination results. Gogo fell ill and Naledi naturally performed all Gogo's chores including baking vetkoek and mealie-bread. Gogo did not want to leave her loyal customers disappointed. One morning, at around 2am Gogo woke up in a sweat. She complained of having difficulty in breathing and began removing her light night dress to ease the heaviness that she felt on her chest. Naledi called for an ambulance and tended to Gogo until the paramedics arrived. The twins were woken by Gogo's screams and Naledi instructed them to look out the window for the ambulance. She did not want them to suffer mental anguish by seeing Gogo in this state of health. The paramedics arrived just after 3am, although Lesedi felt it took them more than two hours to reach their home. By this time, Gogo's breathing was very shallow and she was not responding to Naledi or the paramedics. Naledi held Gogo's hand when her eyes opened for the last time. She squeezed Gogo's hand and told her how much she loved her and thanked her for all the sacrifices she made for the twins and her. Gogo's eyes rolled back and the absence of the rise and fall of her chest indicated that her breathing had stopped. The paramedics immediately noticed this and tried to resuscitate Gogo but their swift attempt was not fruitful. Gogo was dead.

The day before her exam result was due, Lesedi's father suffered a heart attack while at the bakery. He was sixty-one years old and in relatively good health but he had been complaining of chest pain since a fortnight before, but chose to evade the doctor. Mr. Biyela had white coat syndrome since he was a child. Under the guise of a busy work schedule, he avoided any medical check-up. Lesedi suffered a panic attack upon hearing of the death of her father. Things fell apart quickly after that. Another bakery opened near theirs, and their prices were competitive. Rumour had it that the owner of the new bakery was a close friend of Mr. Biyela's oldest sister and she was an investor in the business. Sales began to dwindle at Biyela's Delights. Mrs Biyela could not afford to pay for the upkeep of their luxurious family home. They were forced to rent a more affordable two-bedroom apartment with one bathroom, in a suburb about thirty kilometres away from their former home.

Minnie assisted her Mum and sister financially, but she also had other financial commitments. She and Moses were planning on marrying on an estate in Ballito and honeymooning in Paris for a month. Minnie dreamt of having a garden wedding since she was a little girl and had always wanted to tour Paris after seeing many movies that were filmed in Paris.

Then came a shocking revelation – Lesedi failed her examination. She did not qualify to write the supplementary exam and did not have the motivation to repeat the academic year, much to the dismay of her ambitious sister. She eventually got a job as a receptionist at a law firm called Reed and Associates, but only because Minnie was friends with one of the senior partners. If only she had invested more time in her studies, she would have been a highly paid lawyer.

Naledi was head hunted by a popular law firm, Reed and Associates. She was offered a lucrative package and the benefits were too good to turn down. The twins were enrolled in a school near her office, and she hired an au pair to care for them after school. The chagrin that Lesedi felt each time she saw Naledi, who was dressed in the latest designer wear was palpable. Everyone at the office knew that Lesedi was envious of Naledi. She would make snide remarks about Naledi to the other administrative staff, once even referring to 'new money,' a term coined for people who recently became wealthy. Naledi killed Lesedi with her kindness. When she cleaned out her closet, she gave Lesedi some of the clothes, shoes and bags that she no longer made use of. Lesedi was dumbstruck but managed to utter an almost inaudible 'thank you.' On rainy days, Naledi would offer Lesedi a lift to the bus stop which was quite a distance from the firm. Lesedi's mindset towards Naledi changed and she never gossiped about her again. The two weren't friends but they were amicable.

Naledi is glad that she studied hard at university. The world is now her oyster! Lesedi wishes she was as diligent as Naledi.

13
CHOICES
ख∕फ

Shaun Fynn was a thug. That was according to his inquisitive neighbour, Mel, who was in regular contact with his mother and who voluntarily kept an eye on the goings on at the Fynn's home. Shaun was friends with delinquents and hated school. None of the parents in the neighbourhood wanted Shaun to date their daughters.

They say that an apple doesn't fall too far from the tree. In Shaun's case, that saying does not ring true. Shaun's parents were professional and forthright people. They were also kind, generous and very loving. Shaun's parents fed the homeless people in town every alternate Saturday and naturally their popularity within their community grew.

Shaun's younger brother, Christopher, was the head prefect and applied to study Mechanical Engineering at the University of Cape Town. Christopher wanted to become an engineer since he was five years old. His parents thought that he would change his career choice as he grew older, but they were wrong. Christopher was studious and was often disheartened when he achieved anything less than an 'A' on any test. If they didn't bear a striking similarity, their teachers would never have believed that they were biological brothers.

Shaun struggled to concentrate in class. No matter how often and earnestly he tried to study, he could not grasp the lessons taught to him, and there came a time when he just gave up on studying. When his concerned grade nine form teacher called a meeting with his parents, they immediately sought a tutor for him and made an appointment to see their family doctor regarding his concentration problem. They spared no cost in getting their eldest child the help that he needed.

Mr. Fynn placed an advert in the local newspaper for a tutor and twelve people responded. After Mr and Mrs Fynn met with the applicants and contacted their references for recommendations, Neal was finally chosen. Neal was a twenty-one year old dark skinned and tall gentleman with dark curly hair, and was studying towards a Bachelor of Actuarial Science degree. He had tutored high school pupils since leaving school. He was a sought after tutor because he passed matric with an A aggregate and achieved the highest marks for Maths and Science in his school in the matric examination. When Neal began tutoring Shaun, he had been on Ritalin for two weeks, as prescribed his doctor.

Neal had tutored pupils with various conditions such as attention deficit disorder, attention deficit hyperactivity disorder, depression and anxiety; so, he was patient with Shaun and always spoke to him calmly.

Within the first two and a half months of receiving tuition from Neal, Shaun's parents and teachers noticed that his results were improving. They were pleased. Shaun's Mum bought him a new cellular phone as an incentive, but his behaviour changed.

Shaun became withdrawn at school and home and also lost his appetite. He would always look forward to indulging in his Mum's mouth-watering curries and roasts and he would never refuse a generous helping of his grandmother's banana loaf, but now he simply refused to eat his favourite food.

Neal was often a witness to Shaun's sudden outbursts, and it became increasingly difficult to tutor or trust him when money went missing from his wallet and when he did not take the initiative to do any homework. At one tutoring session, Neal had R400 in his wallet, which was kept in his briefcase. He was at the cashier, paying for a Coke and pie after tutoring Shaun, when he saw that there was only R200 in his wallet. Neal thought that maybe he was mistaken about the actual amount that was in his wallet. The next time that Neal visited the Fynn's home, he counted the money in his wallet thrice.

There was R550. When he reached home, Neal immediately counted the money and found that only R250 was in the wallet. Shaun must have stolen the money while Neal used the loo, yet he continued to tutor Shaun because he really wanted him to succeed. Neal just ensured that he left his wallet in his car when he tutored Shaun. However, after an astonishing incident one Tuesday afternoon, Neal did not return. Shaun greeted Neal with a warm smile at the door and invited him in, welcomingly. Neal welcomed the change in Shaun because of the strenuous prior weeks. As Neal took his seat at the study desk, Shaun opened his pencil case and cockroaches crept out of the case. Neal isn't sure how many cockroaches were in the case, but there were definitely more than three. Shaun placed the cockroaches in the pencil case to scare off Neal. It worked. Neal let out three continuous screams and Christopher ran into the study upon hearing the clamour. Christopher saw his brother pick up a cockroach and fling it on Neal's face.

"Shaun! Stop it!" Christopher shouted to his brother, "Or, I'm going to call Mum."

"Go ahead you tattletale," said Shaun.

At that moment, Neal ran out the door taking his bag of books and tutoring notes.

"I'm leaving and I'm never coming back here," said Neal as he stormed out.

Christopher ran after him. He hated conflict and wanted to placate Neal.

"Wait! Please, just wait," Christopher called out to Neal.

"Your brother is on a downward spiral. I can't help him anymore"

Christopher apologised on his brother's behalf and promised to get his parents to ring him to discuss Neal's behaviour.

"That won't be necessary. I have given up on your brother. He knew that I have a fear of cockroaches because I previously discussed my arachnophobia with him."

Shaun's parents were livid. They tried to reach out to Neal, but he refused to take their calls. Shaun scraped a pass in grade nine, but his parents knew that without Neal, he had a slim chance of passing grade ten. They did find another tutor, but she quickly abandoned her tutoring duties after Shaun put a dead lizard in her coffee. Mr and Mrs Fynn did not bother getting another tutor for their delinquent son.

Unbeknown to the Fynns, Shaun had met two men at one of the feeding schemes that his parents ran. The men begged on the street all day and used all the money that they received to buy drugs. The enormity of struggling at school weighed heavily on Shaun. He guilelessly confided in the two men who offered him a quick fix that would numb his emotional pain and aid him to study. They claimed the drug would send him into a euphoric state and he would have increased energy to cope with his schoolwork. Shaun was not aware that these treacherous men recruited young men to buy drugs and believed them. The drug lords rewarded the men by giving them drugs at no cost.

When Shaun first sniffed cocaine he felt his senses explode and he was more energetic. After his third hit, Shaun was hooked. He made plans to meet both men or one of the men either before school, after school or on weekends. He found it difficult to control his emotions when he did not get his fix or when the men did not deliver the drugs on time. The allowance money that he received was used to feed his sinful habit. When his parents cut back on his allowance after the cockroach incident, he sold his PlayStation and Xbox to pay for the drugs. When Christopher asked Shaun where their gaming equipment was, he told him that a friend had asked to borrow it. He blatantly lied and became aggressive when he was questioned by his brother. After a month, Christopher insisted that Shaun ask his friend to return the PlayStation and Xbox. Shaun told him that his friend had a burglary and the items were stolen. As days went by, Christopher noticed that the television set in Shaun's room had disappeared. Once again, Shaun told Christopher that he lent it to a friend.

The domestic worker, Helena, had noticed the disappearance of the items, but she did not want to get Shaun into trouble. After all, she had a soft spot for him since she cared for him since he was three months old. She bathed him, fed him and changed his diapers when his Mum returned to work after maternity leave. Helena would not let Shaun down, although she did sense that something was not right with the boy. He did not seem like himself lately, but she could not pinpoint exactly what the problem was. She initially thought that the change in his behaviour was due to his disappointment in himself due to his poor academic performance or because he was jealous of his brilliant brother, but something made her believe those were not the reasons for his strange behaviour. Helena was determined to get to the bottom of this issue, and she knew exactly when she would do this – when Mr and Mrs Fynn were at work and the boys were at school. She also knew exactly where to start looking – the white and grey locked drawer beside Shaun's bedside. Shaun usually never locked it, but lately the drawer was always locked. What was Shaun hiding there?

The next morning, while she had the house to herself, Helena began her search. She knew that Shaun kept the key to the locked draw on the top layer of his shoe rack. Shaun trusted Helena with this knowledge. She found the silver key and opened the drawer. To her surprise, she found a see-through plastic bag filled with a powdery white substance. She opened the bag and felt the substance. She knew what it was. Her previous employer, Mr Henry, was a cocaine addict. He snorted cocaine, sometimes in her presence, for many years before he died of a heart attack. Helena did not abandon her job because she needed the income. Mr Henry was a chartered accountant and paid her handsomely. Helena at the time, was in her early twenties and had two children to support. Both children lived with her unemployed husband. Her husband was a petrol attendant, but he was caught in the crossfire of a shootout between police and hijackers. Due to his severe injuries from the shooting, his leg had to be amputated, and he subsequently lost his job.

Helena placed the plastic bag in her dress pocket. She was fond of Shaun, but she had to inform Mrs Fynn about her finding in the hope that she would intervene. Helena wanted to approach Mrs Fynn instead of Mr Fynn, because she felt more comfortable talking to her.

That afternoon, while Mrs Fynn was preparing supper, Helena showed her the bag of cocaine found in Shaun's bedroom. Mrs Fynn almost dropped her cooking spoon on the floor. She took the bag from Helena and poured out its contents on the kitchen counter.

"This is definitely cocaine," said Mrs Fynn.

"I know. I think Shaun is taking drugs. It would explain his sudden change of behaviour," Helena proclaimed.

Mrs Fynn just looked at the cocaine and began shaking her head, wondering where did she go wrong as a parent.

"I have to inform his father… His father has to know about this," Mrs Fynn stammered.

Mr Fynn arrived from work to the bad news. He did not doubt that the cocaine found in Shaun's drawer was indeed for Shaun's use.

"I want him out of this house!" screamed Mr Fynn.

"Arnold, he is our son. He needs our help now more than ever. We can't just shut him out," Mrs Fynn tried to hush her husband.

Mr Fynn stormed out the room and made his way to Shaun's room.

The door was locked. He banged on the door repeatedly until Shaun opened it.

"What do you want?" asked Shaun.

"I know that you are on drugs. I want you to get out of this house," his father retorted.

"Fine. I can't wait to get out of this miserable house anyway," screamed Shaun.

Mrs Fynn came running up the stairs and instructed Shaun to pack his clothes. She would take him to her mother's home. His granny, Penny, affectionately known as 'Granny P' would never want to see him living on the streets. She would set him on the straight and narrow path. He was one of the very few people that Shaun listened to at this stage of his life.

Shaun's non-judgmental granny welcomed him lovingly. It pained her to see her favourite grandchild in a horrible state. She sent him to a rehabilitation facility, and he returned to his granny's home after six months. He returned to school, and she insisted on dropping him off and fetching him from school. She also cooked his favourite food, gave him endless pep talks and confiscated his cellular phone because she did not want him to contact the drug dealers.

Sadly, Shaun relapsed after failing an English test. One of the older boys at his school purchased the drugs for him on credit. At the end of the month, when Shaun did not repay them, they broke into his granny's house at night, tied her to a chair and sealed her mouth with duct tape. They then proceeded to beat Shaun to a pulp. A neighbour who returned from working the graveyard shift at a manufacturing plant, called the police when he saw three men in balaclavas leaving the house. When the police arrived, they freed Shaun's granny and rushed to his aid. His face was swollen, blood oozed from his nose and he could not speak. Granny P had no visible injuries, but she complained of sore wrists and ankles. Shaun's parents arrived shortly thereafter. They could barely recognise their son. They drove him to the nearest hospital, where medical staff attended to him promptly.

"Who would want to harm Shaun?" Mrs Fynn mused as they were seated in the main reception area of the hospital.

"The one guy kept asking for payment for the drugs. They wanted R500," replied Granny P.

"We need to tell the police. What if they come back to your home?" said Mr Fynn.

"No, don't get the police involved. They might arrest Shaun for taking drugs," Granny P pleaded.

Mr Fynn pondered for a moment.

"Okay, but you are coming to stay with us for a while. I am concerned about your safely," he demanded.

Granny P did not refuse, just to keep the peace.

A CT scan revealed that Shaun sustained multiple facial bone fractures, although there was no damage to his brain. Doctors hospitalised him and advised his parents that due to the extent of his injuries, he would hopefully recover in about four to six weeks.

Granny P stayed with the Fynns for two months, but she missed being in the privacy of her own home. She nursed Shaun back to good health and when he returned to school, she went back home.

Shaun was so traumatised from the beating that he vowed never to use drugs again. He just went cold turkey.

Shortly before Christmas, Granny P's neighbours were awoken by the sound of gunshots and blood curdling screams. They were too scared to venture out, and immediately called the police. Granny P sustained fatal gunshot wounds to her head and chest. The intruders entered by breaking in through the back door. They left a note that read: *"We killed your Granny because you did not pay us the money."*

The Fynns knew what this meant. Granny P's death was a revenge killing. They revealed all to the police, but unfortunately the killers were never found despite an intense investigation. It was rumoured that the drug lords paid the investigating officer a bribe, but nobody knows if there is truth to that accusation. Shaun was distraught because he blamed himself for Granny P's death. Although he was in mourning, he was determined to make a success out of his life.

He went to trade school and eventually became a plumber, just like his grandfather. He worked at Mike's plumbing before starting his own plumbing business. While working at Mike's plumbing, he fell in love with Shanice, who was the receptionist. The couple eventually married and had a pigeon pair. Shaun named his daughter after his grandmother. He knew Granny P would have been proud.

14
SEPARATED
∂℘

*L*aura's heart aches when she sees the white and blue aeroplane take off. She feels disheartened, yet she's unable to cry. When the aeroplane is out of sight, she walks away from the viewing window, although her legs can hardly carry her. Around her there are hundreds of people, but she is oblivious of them. In her car, away from the hustle and bustle, she puts her head on the steering wheel and lets out all the tears. Laura's sister, Amy, was on that aeroplane. Amy was jetting off to New York to be an au pair. She signed a two-year contract with an American au pair agency four months prior. Their parents, Kirk and Louise, opted not to come to the airport because they hated goodbyes. They knew that they would ball their eyes out and Amy hated attention being drawn to her.

Laura returned to the apartment that she and Amy shared and gazed around. Just a few days earlier, she was helping Amy to pack for America. After the girls completed school, they decided to move out of their parent's home. Laura and Amy secured jobs as waitresses at Fred's Fantastic Fries and Frappes. They were therefore able to afford to rent a two-bedroom flat in the city. Amy promised to continue to send her share of the rent every month so that Laura could continue to afford to live in the flat. Amy missed Kirk and Louise just as much as Laura did, and the girls visited their childhood home every Sunday afternoon for Louise's delicious roast beef, gravy, creamy spinach and honey glazed carrots. Louise always gave them snacks to take home and Kirk lovingly gave them spending money even though they were both earning an income.

"Why can't you work as an au pair in South Africa?" Laura asked when Amy told her that she would be leaving to America in five months.

"I want to travel the world Laurie and meet new people. I also want to make enough money to buy a home one day. You should consider coming to America too."

Amy called her sister 'Laurie' and Laura called Amy 'Aims' since they were children. Those nicknames stuck throughout the years.

Laura raised her eyebrows.

"Aims, you know I can't!"

Laura had a fear of flying and she was claustrophobic. She also got terribly homesick when she and Amy went on a two-night excursion to the Drakensburg when they were sixteen. Living in another country was out of the question.

Amy and Laura were twins who were born twenty minutes apart in a Pietermaritzburg hospital. Their mother, Tracey, a high school learner was seventeen years old when she birthed them and was shunned by her family because she fell pregnant out of wedlock. Their father had deserted their mother upon hearing that she was pregnant, and she therefore had no financial or emotional support, with the exception of a few friends who rallied around her after the birth of the girls. It was 1988 and most people were conservative thinkers. Tracey decided to put them up for adoption when they were six months old, because she felt that they deserved a better life. She was living with her best friend, Retha and Retha's family, who allowed her to use their spare room. She no longer wanted to burden Retha and her family, although they assured her that they were happy to help until she found a job. Tracey called a social worker and the girls were removed from her care. Her only request was that the girls' adoptive parents kept their names. Amy and Laura were named after their biological great grandmothers.

Durbanites Kirk and Louise were married for ten years before Louise fell pregnant. Kirk was a greengrocer and Louise was a housewife. Both were in their early forties. Unfortunately, Louise suffered a miscarriage and became severely depressed thereafter. After the initial miscarriage, she fell pregnant again, but also miscarried. The couple decided to adopt to complete their family and after many rounds of interviews with a social worker, the couple were informed that Amy and Laura were up for adoption. Their prayers had been answered. Since they were twins, they decided to adopt them both. Louise spent a few weeks getting the nursery ready and Kirk bought age-appropriate toys and clothes for the girls. They decided that the twins would share a room until they were much older. The social worker was impressed at the effort that they had made to win the girls over and make them feel comfortable. The twins' first night at their new home was very eventful. Amy and Laura wailed throughout the night and had difficulty falling asleep. Louise and Kirk tried to soothe them by rocking them to sleep, giving them a warm bath and even singing to them, but the girls continued to cry. The couple barely slept. Luckily, Kirk had taken leave from work for two weeks. It took about a month for the twins to get settled into a routine. Kirk and Louise were exhausted after that first month, but they were grateful for the girls who brought them much joy. After all, they had waited more than a decade to be parents. One would never say that Kirk and Louise were not Amy and Laura's biological parents because they doted on them since they first met. Amy and Laura showed nothing but love and affection to Kirk and Louise. Of course, they did have off days on which they would have tantrums and become moody, but mostly they were loving children.

When the girls were twelve years old, Kirk and Louise told them about the adoption. Amy took the news well, but Laura did not. She felt that for twelve years, Kirk and Louise had lied to them, therefore their whole life was a lie. Laura kept asking who else knew the truth, so that she knew who else could not be trusted. Although Laura did not want to talk to her adoptive parents, they still doted on her. When Laura did not want to have dinner with the rest of the family, Louise would take her food to her bedroom. When Kirk went on shopping trips with Amy, he would not forget to buy Laura something too. Eventually, Laura came round and forgave her parents for withholding the secret. After the revelation, Laura became more attached to Amy. The twins always shared a close bond, although their personalities were different. Since Amy was extroverted, she took drama and ballet lessons. Laura was introverted and took art and music lessons. Suddenly, Laura insisted on joining Amy's drama classes. Their parents did not object, although they did think it was odd. Since the girls took different classes, they had different groups of friends. When Amy had sleepovers at her friend, Nicole's home, Laura insisted on going with her. Laura also hated shopping trips because she did not like being around too many people. After the revelation, Laura accompanied her adoptive parents and Amy on all shopping trips. Only when Amy moved to America did Laura begin to come out of her shell.

Laura missed her sister immensely and she tried to avoid going to places that they frequented together because it would bring back memories of her sister. Although, these memories were mostly good, Laura could not handle the fact that she would not see her sister for the next two years. The visit would cost her a small fortune, and she was determined to pay for the entire visit herself. Laura had an inkling that Amy would never return to South Africa. Her fate would be the same as Denise Van der Merwe, the daughter of Kirk's best friend. Denise studied hotel and tourism management, and when an opportunity arose for her to work at a world famous ski resort in Colorado, she accepted. A tall and handsome chef at the resort caught the eye of Denise in her fifth month in the land of the free. His name was Jackson Wilson, and he looked like a younger version of Denzel Washington. Denise and Jackson ended up working the same shift and the two quickly realised that they had many hobbies and interests in common. Jackson had a quirky sense of humour, was well-mannered, wise and he loved traveling. Their first date was at a diner not too far from the resort. After two dates, Jackson officially asked Denise to be his girlfriend. She was ecstatic and instinctively knew that he was 'The One.'

For many months, Denise grappled with how she was going to tell her parents about Jackson, especially because he belonged to a different race group. Before she left home, her father remined her that Schalk was eagerly awaiting her return so that he could marry her. Schalk, a twenty-six year old red haired lad from Mpumalanga had seen Denise at a wedding and enquired about her relationship status from one of her cousins. When Schalk learned that Denise was single, he struck a conversation with her. She was not attracted to him, but was too polite to refuse an invitation to supper at a pizza place. Denise felt that he was chauvinistic and a narcissist, but when she voiced her concerns to her father, he insisted that Schalk would be able to take care of her and he would fit in with their family. Secretly, Denise hoped that Schalk would forget about her in two years. Less than a year after that conversation, Denise was anxious about another conversation that she needed to have with her parents, and one that could no longer be put off. Denise chose a Friday afternoon to reveal the news to her parents. She knew her parents would be mellow and relaxed because they usually enjoyed a few glasses of wine while braaiing. Friday was braai day at the Van der Merwe's home. Lamb, chicken and sausages were always on the menu. Although Denise's parents were relaxed, they did not take the news well.

"What about Schalk? Isn't he perfect for you?" her father asked.

"Papa, I don't love Schalk. I can't imagine a life with him. Jackson is the one for me," Denise replied.

Her parents were flabbergasted and wondered what was so special about Jackson that would make their daughter fall head over heels in love with him.

"Maybe I can bring Jackson to South Africa with me when I visit?" Denise suggested.

Her parents point blankly refused, but time changed their stance on the matter. When Jackson visited South Africa, the Van der Merwe's grew to love him and they saw how well he treated their daughter. Denise was truly happy and wanted to spend the rest of her life with Jackson. After receiving their parents' blessings, Jackson and Denise were married in a quaint chapel in New York. The couple chose not to have children immediately because they wanted to travel the word before they could start a family.

Laura wished that she could have a family of her own in years to come. She hoped that she would have twin daughters who would have a close bond like she and Amy did. Louise saw that her daughter was often melancholic, and decided that she should assist Laura in tracking down her biological parents. Amy vocalised that she did not want to find her biological parents, but since the day that Laura found out that she was adopted, she wanted to.

"I wonder what our real Mum looked like. I wish I could see a picture of her. I wonder if she is still alive?" Laura would say when they were teenagers.

"Shoosh! Don't let Mum and Dad hear you say that," Amy protested. Amy did not want to hurt the feelings of her adoptive parents.

Kirk and Louise overheard the girls speak about their biological parents on numerous occasions, and knew that the day would come when at least one of the girls would want to find them. The time had come for them to help Laura with this mission. Louise contacted the social work department and was given the numbers of two people who could be of assistance since the social worker who interviewed her eighteen years ago had retired from the profession. Belinda Steenkamp was a short, blonde lady who was instrumental in the mission of finding the twins' biological mother. She looked through old records and found an address and contact number for their Mum. It was now revealed that their Mum's name was Tracey. Louise gave the information to Laura. Immediately, Laura rang the number but it was no longer in service. Early the next morning, they made the trip to the address. They left early because their desired destination was approximately 60 km away.

A gray haired lady who was slightly hunched, answered the door.

"Hello. My name is Laura. I got your address from a social worker. I believe that my mother Tracey lived here," said Laura.

"Oh my goodness! Your mother and I prayed that this day would come," exclaimed the lady.

The lady moved closer to Laura. She did not ask for any proof of identification or further details because Laura was a carbon copy of her biological mother.

"My name is Susan. I'm Tracey's aunt. She is now living in America," she said with a warm smile.

"America!" exclaimed Laura with her jaw hanging.

"Please do come in, ladies. I would love to chat about Tracey. I've just baked a batch of scones," the lady said invitingly.

The ladies were gestured to the white walled lounge where they waited. A few minutes later, Susan appeared with buttered scones and tea.

"You know, Tracey hoped that her daughters would try to find her one day," she said while pouring the tea from a floral jug into white tea cups. "I have a letter from her that I am sure you would love to see. She meant to give it to the social worker but decided against it."

Laura's curiosity piqued. "Please let me read the letter," she said while accepting the cup of tea.

"The letter is in my bedroom next door. I will fetch it for you," Susan replied.

Louise took a sip of the tea. It was too sugary for her liking, but she drank it nonetheless.

"When did my biological mother leave for America?" Laura asked when Susan returned with the letter.

"Three years after you and your sister were born, your father and mother got back together. Your father's parents died and left him a large sum of money. Your father came to South Africa for six months to tend to his parents estate and arrange the funeral. He found your mother and knew that he couldn't let her go. Your father proposed and your Mum accepted. They heard that you and your sister were doing well in your new home and they did not want to break up a happy home."

"So my biological mother and father are married?" Laura asked rhetorically.

Louise was grateful that Tracey decided to give the girls up for adoption so that they could have a better life, but now she feared losing them to their biological mother.

"When last did you see Tracey or her husband?" Louise asked perturbedly.

"They try to visit once every two or three years. Rick owns a hardware store in New York which is always busy. They live in New York too."

"My sister lives in New York. I have to tell her," said Laura before taking her cellphone out of the bag.

Louise persuaded her not to. "There's plenty of time to call your sister, my dear. Why don't you read the letter first?" Louise wanted to know the contents of the letter. She was eager to know what Tracey had to tell the twins.

Laura opened the letter. Her mother's handwriting was immaculate. The paper on which it was written was slightly faded, but Laura could still decipher the contents, she then read the letter out aloud:

> *My darling girls, Amy and Laura (I hope that your new parents kept the names that I chose for you).*

I am writing this letter with a heavy heart. It pains me to give you girls away, but I believe that you will be in safe hands. Your new family will give you a life that I believe you deserve. I am eighteen years old and your father has unfortunately ended our relationship. I met your father when I was fifteen and although his parents did not approve of our relationship, we would meet secretly. His parents sent him to America when they found out that I was pregnant in the hope that he would forget about me. Your father is a loving and caring man, although his actions didn't always align with his words. I truly hope that one day, if our circumstances permit, we will all meet and forge a great relationship.

I will love you both forever.

Your Mum,

Tracey

Laura held the letter to her chest and gathered her thoughts.

The trio spent hours talking about Tracey and her husband.

"I want to contact my biological mother," Laura said.

"I'm so glad that you do, darling. I would be happy to help," Susan replied.

Susan gave Laura the contact details and she promised to visit again.

When Laura reached home, she immediately rang her sister. Laura needed Amy, more than ever, for the last part of this mission.

"Amy, you are not going to believe this! Our biological Mum is living in New York," Laura said before the call got cut due to bad cellphone reception.

15

WHEN HARRY MET TRUDY
୬୦

𝓗arry Stoffels was a forty-one-year-old bachelor. He never married because he was uber fussy and fastidious, and so he lived alone in a one-bedroom apartment in Mitchells Plain. His mother and three siblings tried to set him up on many dates but he always found faults with the women.

"What is wrong with Sandra? She is good-looking and financially independent," his seventy-year-old Mum protested.

"Ma, all she talks about is money. The first thing she asked me is how much I make."

"What about Melissa? I feel that you and her have so much in common. There is also Kate, you know. She may seem like a Miss Priss, but she really is a sweetheart."

"Melissa is morbidly obese, Ma. I am not in the least bit attracted to her. Don't even get me started on Kate…." Harry went on and on.

Mrs Stoffels knew what the reason behind her son's fault finding was.

"You're never going to find another Nellie," she told her son.

At the mention of Nellie's name, Harry stopped speaking and he lowered his head.

"She's married now, Harry. It's time to move on."

Harry walked to the floral two-seater sofa, plonked himself on the two-seater and placed his head in his hands.

Upon hearing this fact for the countless time, Harry felt like a million nails were piercing through his body. The pain was unbearable. He just got up and left without even kissing his mother goodbye.

Nellie was Harry's first love. She had light brown eyes, black hair and an infectious bubbly personality. It was love at first sight when the teenagers first laid eyes on each other. Harry met her at his cousin, Cindy's, sweet sixteen birthday party. Their fathers were brothers. Harry was the only cousin invited to Cindy's party since they were close in age and got on well. Nellie was his cousin's best friend and delivered a commendable speech at the rose themed party. Harry was seventeen and quite the looker too, but he was an introvert. He was tall with almond shaped green eyes and olive skin. When Nellie spoke, she looked at Harry only. He too, could not stop staring at the attractive stranger. Nellie ended her speech with a quote from William Shakespeare, "A friend is one that knows you as you are, understands where you have been, accepts what you have become, and still gently allows you to grow."

Harry knew that he had to talk to the beautiful stranger before the party was over, but there were so many dashing young men who also vied for her attention, that every time he tried to walk over to talk to her, somebody beat him to it. The other men were like vultures to meat.

"Nellie asked me to give you her number. I think she has a crush on you. She keeps asking about you," Cindy said when all the guests had left. She found her cousin in the living room helping himself to shredded chicken and cheese rolls and non-alcoholic punch. Harry was shy to eat in front of the watchful eyes of the others at the party.

"Really? I have been trying to talk to her this whole time," Harry responded with excitement.

Harry took the piece of paper with Nellie's number scribbled on.

"Well then, you better call her tonight," Cindy advised her favourite cousin.

"What do I say to her?" asked a thrilled but nervous Harry.

"I don't know. You're smart. You will think of something to say to her. She did ask if you had a girlfriend."

"Tell me more about her," Harry pleaded.

"Well, she lives with her dad and step-mum. Her parents divorced when she was three. She has a half-brother. Her favourite singer is Whitney Houston and she loves pizza."

Harry took a sip of punch as he listened to his outspoken cousin. He then placed the cup on the kitchen counter.

"…and you are sure she doesn't have a boyfriend?" Harry asked.

"Would she ask about you and give you her number if she had a boyfriend? Don't be silly, Harry!" Cindy placed her hands on her hips as she spoke to Harry. She was known to be dramatic.

"Okay, okay! I will call her tonight," Harry assured her.

Harry prayed that her father or step-mum didn't answer as he dialled her number. When Nellie answered, he was relieved. The two spoke for about half an hour and made plans to meet for burgers and milkshake at Wimpy that weekend.

On that first date, Harry fell for her hook, line and sinker. On their second date, he made his feelings known and asked her to officially be his girlfriend.

Mrs Stoffels knew that her son was in love because he was always smiling when he spoke to Nellie over the phone and couldn't stop speaking about his new girlfriend to his sisters and friends.

Their date at Wimpy would be the first of many dates they would go on in their five-year relationship. Their love grew stronger and every year they would go to the same Wimpy for lunch. Harry and Nellie were the cutest item in their neighbourhood. They were besotted with each other, would finish each other's sentences and only had eyes for each other.

After school, Harry worked as a mechanic and Nellie worked as a hairdresser. The couple knew that they would eventually marry each other one day; so, upon receiving their first salaries, they began saving for their big day. Harry was not able to save as much as Nellie because he earned much less than she did, but at that time, Harry's lack of affluence was not an issue for Nellie. Harry never formally proposed to her, but they both often spoke about their life together and the wedding that they wanted. Their guest list was set at one hundred and they decided that they wanted a lamb on spit to be served for the main meal. Their wedding cake was going to be a three-tier chocolate cake covered in white fondant topped with a miniature bride and groom. Vanilla ice-cream and chocolate sauce would be eaten for dessert since it was the first dessert that they shared together. Naturally, Cindy would be the maid of honour, because she was Nellie's best friend. Nellie wanted an off-the-shoulder white wedding dress with silver heels. The couple decided that they wanted to go to Knysna for their honeymoon since both had never been there. All that needed to be decided on was the date and venue.

Business bloomed at the salon where Nellie worked, so her boss decided to open another branch at Sea Point. Nellie's spinster aunt lived near Sea Point and insisted that she stay with her during the week. Crime was rife at the time and she did not want Nellie to travel late. On most days, the salon closed at 7pm to accommodate those who could not make it to the salon during the day. A man was murdered in a taxi early that year and everybody in the area were now taking extra precaution to ensure their safety. Harry offered to drop her off at work and fetch her, but she thought it would be too costly and time consuming for him. They were still saving towards the wedding and every cent counted. So, they both agreed that she would stay with her aunt during the week and on Friday evenings, her aunt would drop her off at Mitchells Plain. Early on Monday mornings, either Harry or her father would drop her off at the salon. The routine worked well, until Harry had to work longer hours and Patrick appeared.

Patrick was a new client at the salon. He was a thirty-year old businessman and although he was average looking, he was always well groomed. He drove a flashy BMW and the apartment that he lived in alone, was big enough for at least a family of four. Nellie soon became his favourite hairdresser because of her attention to detail and her friendly demeanour. Patrick often took his clients out for lunch or dinner, and he often asked Nellie to accompany him to these lunch or dinner meetings. She politely refused every time. She made it known that she was engaged and her fiancé would not like the idea of her going out with other men, even if it was in a group. The sly Patrick, devised a plan to win Nellie over. He would buy her expensive gifts every time he visited the salon and he would send her spa vouchers. Nellie could not refuse the gifts and vouchers because he was a high paying client and her boss insisted that she accept the gifts and be cordial to him. Nellie would give all the gifts to her aunt, and simply threw the vouchers away.

That year, Nellie's birthday was on a Thursday. She did not have any major plans for the day, besides a homemade dinner with her aunt. She secretly wished that Harry would visit, but he had to work late. He promised to take her out on a picnic that weekend. Patrick found out her address from one of the ladies at her work and showed up at her house that evening with flowers, a pair of diamond earrings and take-out from her favourite Chinese restaurant. Nellie appreciated the gesture, but she thought it was highly inappropriate. It was her aunt who encouraged her to be nice to Patrick. Secretly, she did not approve of Harry as a husband for her niece.

As the weeks went by, Nellie and Patrick grew close because Harry was always working late and too tired to spend time with her. Nellie was vexed when Harry even forgot the fifth anniversary of their first date, and she struggled to forgive him. Nellie began to develop romantic feelings for Patrick around this time and since she felt that Harry was always working and did not pay enough attention to her, she broke off their engagement. Harry did not take the break-up well. He fell into deep depression and attempted suicide by overdosing on approximately twenty Panado tablets. Luckily, his Mum found him past out on the couch and called for help. Harry initially found it difficult to move on. The teetotaller began drinking alcohol and smoking cigarettes. Nellie was constantly in his thoughts and on the day she married Patrick, he went on a drinking spree with friends to numb the pain. Eventually, Harry stopped drinking, but found it difficult to kick the smoking habit. He had given up on love until Trudy came into his life.

Trudy Fowler was a single mother whose husband, Wesley, was murdered by loan sharks. Wesley had a gambling addiction for which he did not seek help. Almost all the money that he earned from his construction company was spent at various casinos in and around Cape Town. Since she was unemployed, she could not assist Wesley in meeting financial commitments. Her parents assisted them by buying groceries and clothes for their grandchild. Trudy feared for her life and that of her young son when loan sharks visited their home to collect money from Wesley.

"I will pay you back next Friday. I promise," Wesley pleaded with the tall and bulky man.

The other short and stocky man looked at Trudy and her son who were seated in the kitchen. Trudy was terrified.

"Fine, but if the money is not paid to me by next Friday, I will kill your wife and son." The man's eyes widened as he spoke.

Trudy sensed that he was not joking. She heard stories of loan sharks killing an entire family for revenge.

"Nobody is going to kill you and our son. I'm receiving a large sum of money soon. Our debt will be paid," Wesley attempted to reassure her.

Trudy knew when Wesley was lying. He had a habit of biting his lip and not looking her directly in her eyes when the lies spewed out his mouth. She knew that if she believed her husband, she and her son would soon be dead. She ran off to stay with her friend, Rhona in Mitchells Plain. She did not want to tell Wesley where she was staying because she feared that he might come after her and their son. She packed her car, which was a gift from her father, and drove to her friend who welcomed her with open arms. True to his word, the loan shark went to collect his money the following Friday. Wesley did not pay back the money to the loan shark, so he was shot dead. Trudy's mum broke the news to her over the phone. She was grief stricken for a short period, but did not regret her decision to move to Mitchells Plain. She and her son could have been killed too.

Trudy's car broke down one rainy Saturday afternoon, and Rhona advised her to ask Harry Stoffels to repair it. When Trudy first met Harry, her first impression was that he was very handsome and caring, but he seemed to be despondent. Harry heard about Trudy's husband and felt sorry for her. He did not charge her for repairing the car, and she in return invited him for supper to thank him for his kind deed. She won Harry over with her delicious food and warm personality. Harry also enjoyed meeting her son and, in fact, it was her son who asked his Mum repeatedly if "Uncle Harry" could visit over the weekends to play soccer with him. Trudy granted her son's wish. Soon, Harry was visiting every weekend and he fell in love with Trudy and began to share a deep bond with her son. Both, Trudy and Harry did not want to marry, but when Trudy unexpectedly fell pregnant, their parents encouraged them to tie the knot. They married in the presence of fifty loved ones in Harry's Mum's garden. Trudy's son was chosen as the ring bearer. Harry wore a white and black suit and Trudy chose a gold and green dress.

Rose Stoffels was born on a teeth-chattering winter morning. Her rosy cheeks brightened her face and that's how she got her name. She was doted on by her parents and brother. The Stoffel's family was complete and was unbreakable.

Sadly, Patrick eventually left Nellie and ran off with his floozie, Tanya, a twenty-one year old beautician. He showered Tanya with expensive gifts, just as he did to Nellie when they first met. The floozie kept demanding more expensive gifts and Patrick gave in to her demands because he wanted to keep her. He paid no attention to Nellie. Soon, he was staying with the floozie at expensive hotels every weekend. Nellie and their three children were distraught and she pleaded with him to leave Tanya for the sake of their children, but Patrick was too obsessed with the hour glass shaped beauty. He wanted to be with Tanya forever and finally served Nellie with divorce papers. Nellie was furious and hurt. She wanted to seek revenge. She threw paint on Patrick's BMW and broke the windows. It was out of character and she later regretted the incident. Patrick labelled her a 'mad woman' and told her that he wished she was dead.

Nellie moved back to her hometown of Mitchells Plain with her three children. It was there that she bumped into Harry one Saturday morning while shopping at Checkers. She walked up to him and greeted him. The respectable Harry did not really want to converse with Nellie without his wife present. It made him uncomfortable.

"I'm sorry for leaving you all those years ago. It was a mistake," she said with tears in her eyes.

"I forgave you a long time ago, Nellie. I am happier now. I have a wife and two children who bring me much joy," he replied.

Nellie felt a twinge of envy. She did not know that Harry was married. Why hadn't Cindy told her? They were in contact at least once every three months.

"I'm happy that you are happy," Nellie lied.

Nellie tried to keep the conversation flowing but Harry just listened and answered in a few words. Eventually, he looked at his wristwatch and explained that he had to leave.

"Sorry, I'm in a rush. My wife invited some friends for supper. I don't want to be late," Harry said, leaving a remorseful Nellie in the middle of the shopping aisle. As she watched Harry leave, she thought of how different her life would have been if she had married him.

Verity Publishers
©2022